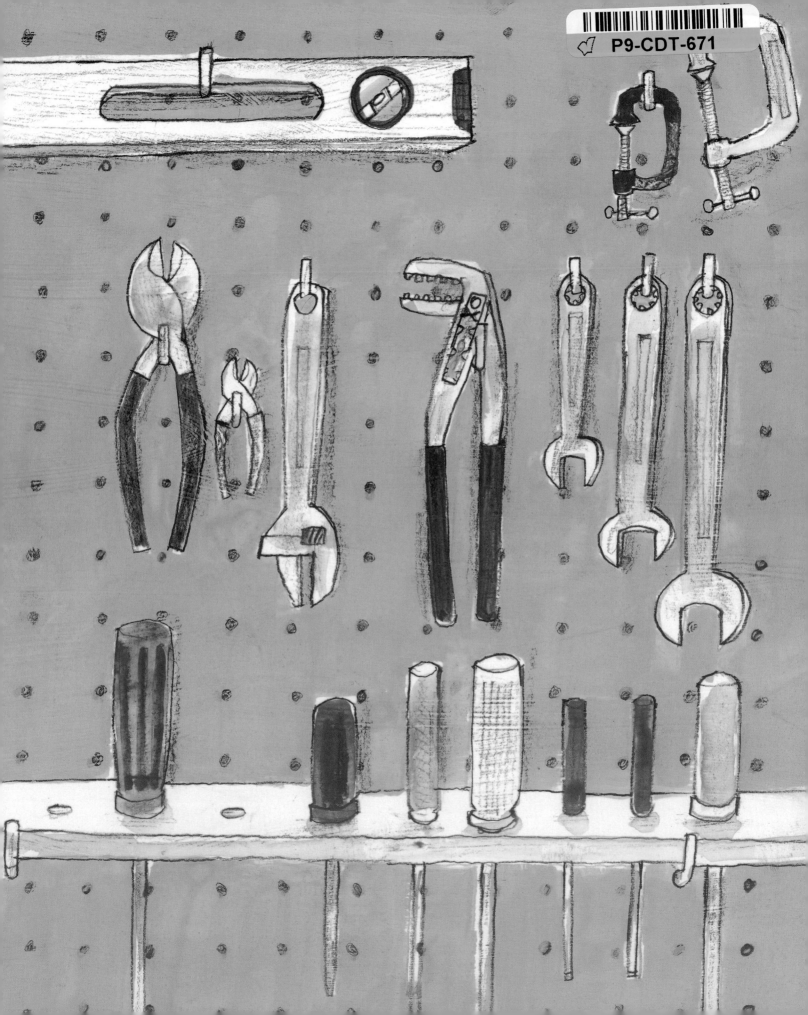

In honor of Ellen Conford and Kate McClellan.
And for Theo Sawyer, a third-generation woodworker. —M.M.

For all the young makers and those who teach them. —G.B.K.

Text copyright © 2021 by Margaret McNamara • Jacket art and interior illustrations copyright © 2021 by G. Brian Karas

All rights reserved. Published in the United States by Schwartz & Wade Books, an imprint of Random House Children's Books, a division of Penguin Random House LLC, New York.

Schwartz & Wade Books and the colophon are trademarks of Penguin Random House LLC.

Visit us on the Web! rhcbooks.com
Educators and librarians, for a variety of teaching tools, visit us at RHTeachersLibrarians.com

Library of Congress Cataloging-in-Publication Data
Names: McNamara, Margaret, author. | Karas, G. Brian, illustrator.
Title: The little library / by Margaret McNamara; illustrated by G. Brian Karas.
Description: First edition. | New York: Schwartz & Wade Books, [2021] |
Series: Mr. Tiffin's classroom | Audience: Ages 4–8. | Audience: Grades K–1. | Summary: Jake, a reluctant reader,
becomes a book lover when the new librarian finds Jake a book about woodworking.
Identifiers: LCCN 2020011696 | ISBN 978-0-525-57833-8 (hardcover) | ISBN 978-0-525-57834-5 (library binding) | ISBN 978-0-525-57835-2 (ebook)
Subjects: CYAC: Books and reading—Fiction. | Libraries—Fiction. | Woodwork—Fiction.
Classification: LCC PZ7.M47879343 Li 2020 | DDC [E]—dc23

The text of this book is set in Century Schoolbook.
The illustrations were rendered in gouache, matte medium, and pencil on paper.
Book design by Rachael Cole

MANUFACTURED IN CHINA
2 4 6 8 10 9 7 5 3 1
First Edition

the little library

by Margaret McNamara
illustrated by G. Brian Karas

schwartz & wade books · new york

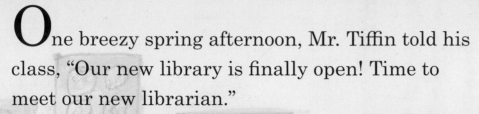

One breezy spring afternoon, Mr. Tiffin told his class, "Our new library is finally open! Time to meet our new librarian."

"I'm excited!" said Jeremy.

"Me too!" said Charlie and Alex together.

"Me three!" said Molly.

"I could stay here and sharpen pencils," said Jake.

Jake was a slow and careful reader. Sometimes he read the same page more than once so he could figure everything out. When it came to Library Day, Jake felt left behind.

The new library smelled like fresh paint and wood.
"Welcome, everybody!" said a friendly-looking person.
"I'm Beck Goode. Please call me Librarian Beck. I'm here
to help you find books to love."

"When you open a book, you open your mind," Elinor announced.

"When *you* open a book," said Jake.

"Why don't you explore the library for a while," said Librarian Beck. "That will help me get to know you."

Kimmy headed to the science section.
Alex and Charlie hunted for a story they could read together.
Tara found the art books and looked for paintings by women.

Jake wandered over to a corner shelf. He studied the bookcase to see how the pieces fit together. He ran his finger along the grooves in the wood.

After a while, Librarian Beck came to talk to him. "See what you think of this," they said.

Librarian Beck put a heavy book into Jake's hands. It was old and worn.

"Woodworking for Young Hands," read Jake.

He opened the book. The first pages were filled with drawings of tools. Jake already knew the names of some of them. "That one's an awl," he said. "My gramps has a workshop."

Jake handed the book back to them. "This has a lot of pictures," he said. "So it doesn't count as reading."

"Says who?" said Librarian Beck.
"A lot of people," said Jake.
"Not me," said Librarian Beck.
Jake checked the book out.

He let it sit for a while when
he got home.
He had other things to do.

After a few days, he read the instructions for the
first project, and the second. They didn't make a lot
of sense to him.

The next Library Day, Jake's book was due back. Slowly, he handed it over.

"The instructions are pretty hard."

"But it looks like you took some good notes," said Librarian Beck. "Want to keep it another week?"

"Sure," Jake said.

Jake spent the next week reading more of the book. Still slowly.

The more he read, the more curious he became about things made of wood.

He looked at the way the three legs of a stool supported the seat.

He noticed that some tables had sharp corners and some were round.

He wondered how
to bend wood to make
the back of a chair.

The next three Library Days, Jake renewed
Woodworking for Young Hands.

Librarian Beck found other books they thought
Jake would like, and Jake checked those out, too.

On a warm sunny morning, Librarian Beck had an
announcement to make. "All library books need to be returned
before the end of school," they said. "That way the library will
be organized and ready when you come back next year."

"Wait," Jake said, "the library is closed all summer?"

"Of course it is," said Robert.

Jake looked down at *Woodworking for Young Hands*. He hadn't realized he'd have to give it back so soon.

That night, Jake had an idea. He turned to a page he had marked in the book. Then he looked around his house.

He found a yardstick,

a screwdriver,

and some three-inch screws.

Then he called Gramps.

Over the next two weekends, Jake spent a lot of time in Gramps's workshop.

Jake measured and marked plywood.

Gramps cut along the lines Jake made.

Gramps drilled holes. Jake screwed in screws.

Jake attached hinges, affixed Plexiglas, and painted.

Gramps and Jake didn't talk a lot while they worked.

They didn't need to.

At last, they were done.

On the last Library Day of the year, Jake brought something very big and very heavy into Mr. Tiffin's classroom. It was covered with a large cloth. "It's for Librarian Beck," he said.

Everyone in the class tried to guess what Jake had made.

"Looks like a giant birdcage," said Charlie.

"It's better than a birdcage," said Jake.

"A dollhouse?" asked Alex.

"Nope," said Jake.

Tara and Jeremy helped carry Jake's surprise into the library. Jake pulled off the cloth.

"It's a little library!" said Jake.

"You built that?" asked Jeremy.

"With help from *Woodworking for Young Hands*," Jake said. "And my gramps."

"What's a little library?" asked Kimmy.

"A little library is a place to share books," said Mr. Tiffin.

"People take a book out and bring it back. Or they replace it with another book," said Librarian Beck. "All for free."

"So while our big library is closed, this little library can stay open," said Jake.

On the very last day of school, after the class
had scrubbed the desks and taken out the trash
and written in the Memory Book, Mr. Tiffin led
them outside.

There was Librarian Beck with the school custodian.
They were standing next to the little library.

"I filled it with books," said Librarian Beck. "Want to
take one out, Jake?" they asked.

"That's okay," said Jake. "I'm going to wait till I can
check out *Woodworking for Young Hands* again next year."

All that summer, Jake's little library stayed busy. People put all kinds of books in and took all kinds of books out.

One hot day in July, a package
arrived for Jake. He tore open
the brown paper. Inside was
Woodworking for Young Hands.

On the first page, he saw this:

Then he saw a note.

Dear Jake,

You loved this book more than anyone had loved it in a long time. "Withdrawn" means this book does not belong to the library anymore. It belongs to you.
See you next year! And keep reading!

— Librarian Beck

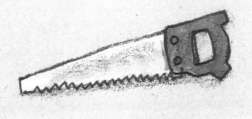

LITTLE FREE LIBRARIES
by Jake

It turns out there are thousands of libraries like the one I made, all over the country and all over the world! They're called Little Free Libraries, and if you want to find out more about them, you can go to LittleFreeLibrary.org. You'll see a ton of information about starting a Little Free Library, from choosing a good spot to asking a grown-up to help keep the library going. You can order a kit from the Little Free Library website, or you can download plans to work from. Your Little Free Library can even appear on an interactive map of the world!

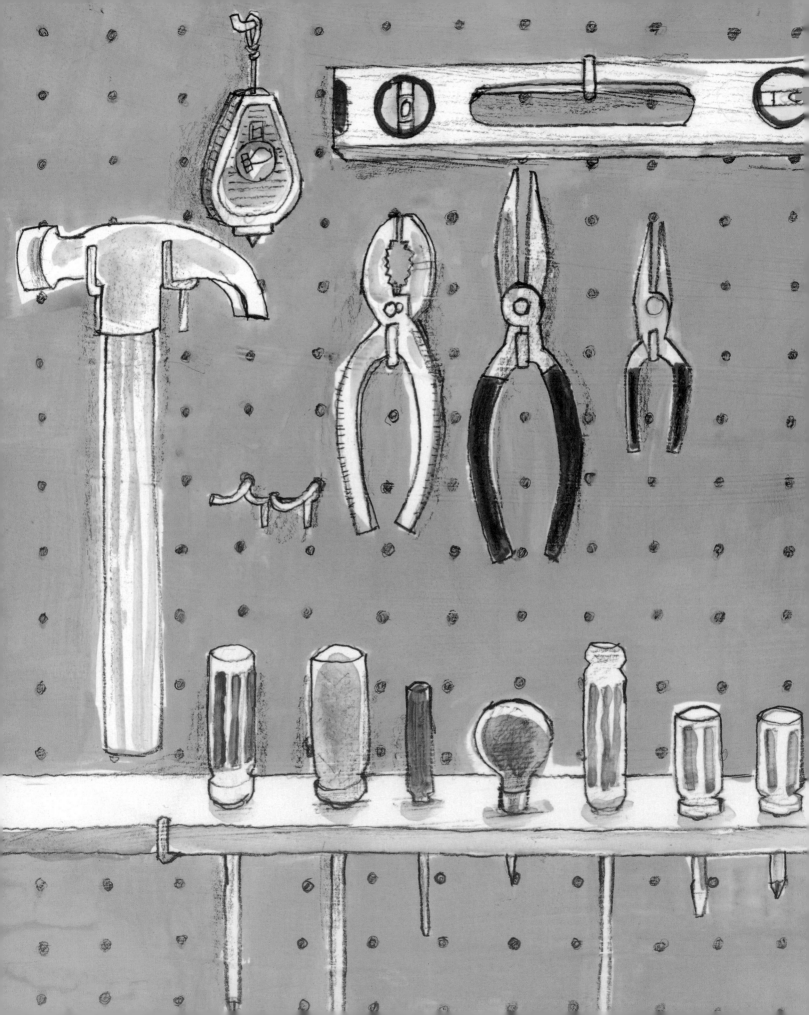